#7:
The Phantom of
Hidden Horse Ranch

by Kristiana Gregory
illustrations by Cody Rutty

Free study guide written by the author with
activities, writing and drawing prompts, a recipe, and
some secrets about Kristiana:
http://kristianagregory.com/

THE PHANTOM OF HIDDEN HORSE RANCH is a work of fiction and is #7 in the Cabin Creek Mysteries series.

Chapters

1
A Bad Sign

*T*he Cabin Creek Shuttle swerved to the side of the mountain road, bumping along the dirt embankment until it skidded to a stop. A police car roared past with its lights blazing and a siren so loud, Claire Posey covered her ears. Her cousins, Jeff and David Bridger, whipped around in their seats to watch two fire trucks speed by, followed by an ambulance. The other passengers craned their necks to look.

Along the right side of the bus, they could see down to Green Meadows. It was a lush valley where farms and pastures spread out like a bumpy quilt. The cousins had seen this vista many times, but today an ominous plume of black smoke billowed into the sky.

"Oh no, Gram's place is near there," said Jeff, worry in his voice. He was twelve. It had been his idea to help their grandparents this summer on the ranch.

Claire tried to look at the fire, but her backpack had slid from her seat. Out spilled her diary, flashlight, and first-aid kit. Though just nine years old, she had organized her clothes into neat little balls that, unfortunately, now unrolled down the aisle.

Frantic that someone might see her package of new underwear, she hurried to retrieve everything.

"Guys?" she said to the brothers in front of her, "I hope that smoke isn't a bad sign."

David frowned. "Me, too. And I hope no one's hurt." He was two years younger than his brother. Unlike Jeff, he had waited until the last minute to get dressed this morning. David's T-shirt was inside out and backwards, the tag in front. His socks were mismatched and his blond hair stood up straight from lack of a comb.

Adults and children in the crowded bus talked among themselves, wondering about the fire. Some tried to make calls on their cell phones, but reception wavered because of the mountainous terrain. When the driver responded to crackling from his two-way radio, everyone leaned forward to listen. The conversation sounded garbled, but at last he said, "Right-o, will do."

He turned to face his passengers. "Folks, one of the ranches is burning and a road is blocked so we need to sit here till they clear it. We're on Overlook Pass, so enjoy the view."

*W*hile waiting for the road to re-open, some adults got off the bus with their cameras. Many unpacked lunches and snacks. David's apple had rolled to the back of the bus and down the sticky stairwell. He rubbed it clean against his shirt then offered it to his older brother.

"Thanks, dude." Jeff had brown hair and brown eyes. He wore sneakers and jeans with a clean T-shirt from *Camp Whispering Pines*. He said, "My sandwich is squished, but it's good. Want half?"

"Yeah. I love salami, just like Grandpa."

Claire opened a baggie of chocolate chip cookies. "Mom said these should last a week, but we may as well eat them now. Hey, look over there. You can see Blue Lake. Is that Lost Island?"

The cousins stared out their windows, which they'd opened for a breeze. In the distance to the south, Grizzly Paw Wilderness bordered a vast lake, sparkly turquoise in the sunshine. Sailboats and water skiers appeared as tiny white dots.

"Yep, sure is!" David answered. "Wouldn't it be cool if we could see some gold from here, you know, reflecting the sun?"

"Totally," said Jeff. "I bet we dig up more coins the next time we're out there and search Robber's Cave."

"Mmm-mum," Claire said, her mouth full of cookie. Her curly red ponytail bounced as she chewed. "Mm, and maybe even when we go camping again at Skull Cliff. The legend says gold could be hidden there, too."

The threesome smiled at one another. They remembered the skeleton they had found on the island earlier this summer, and the treasure at the bottom of Blue Lake. While eating lunch they mused about their discoveries, but also kept a worried eye on the black smoke.

Fortunately the town of Cabin Creek was over the next ridge, safe from the fire. The children's log homes edged the lake in a private cove where they had their own canoes and rowboat. They loved summers. School was out and as long as they did their chores they were free to explore Lost Island. Their Lookout Tower and secret fort were safely hidden on this wooded isle.

A favorite time was visiting their grandparents at Hidden Horse Ranch. The place was nicknamed Lucky Bridger because so many good things happened there. But today, watching smoke fill the peaceful valley, they feared its luck might have run out.

An hour waiting on the bus turned into two. Finally the driver's radio beeped with a report. "Listen up folks," he announced. "The rangers say there's been a terrible incident. I don't know what it is, but we'll just take 'er easy down the mountain." He put his hand on the long gearshift that poked up from the floor, shifted into low then drove back onto the twisty road.

2
Hidden Horse Ranch

*T*he sun was setting behind the mountain as the bus turned onto Bridger Trail Road. It bordered two hundred acres of grassland with a split-rail fence. Far ahead by Gram's sprawling ranch house, there were firefighters in yellow coats. They were rolling up hoses from the pond where apparently water had been pumped. Red lights on the trucks and police car still flashed. The ambulance was gone.

The cousins jumped from their seats.

"Someone's dead, I just know it," David cried.

"Hold on youngsters," said the driver, "we'll be there in a bit."

For several minutes the bus rattled along the washboard road. Finally it pulled to a stop by the standing mailbox. A lamppost glowed with light, illuminating a slab of stone that had been chiseled with the words: *Welcome Friends*.

The kids gathered their backpacks and as soon as the driver opened the door, they bolted down the steps and ran toward the house.

"Grandpa?" they called.

"Gram?"

Though it was dusk, they could see a row of stables smoldering with black steam. A stench of charred wood filled the air.

"What happened to the horses?" yelled Claire. "Where's our Gram?"

A policewoman met them on the brick path leading up to the house. A trellis of roses arched over the porch where they heard the chirping of crickets. The woman held up her hand to stop the children.

"I'm afraid you can't go in," she said.

"What? Why not?" Claire began to cry.

Jeff put a protective arm around her and his younger brother. "We want to see our grandparents," he said.

Just then a large brown dog burst through the screen door, tearing the netting from its frame. He wagged in exuberant greeting.

"Buddy!" the children cried. They hugged his neck and pet him. Then disobeying the officer they hurried into the house. They found several firefighters in the kitchen drinking coffee.

When they saw their grandfather with them, smoking his pipe and chatting, they yelled with relief. "Grandpa!"

11

"Well I'll be." Howard Bridger set his pipe down. Then he opened his arms for a swooping hug, all three at once. "Del honey, the kids are here, safe and in one piece. We were getting worried that the bus slid off the road or something!"

He apologized to the policewoman who had followed the kids. "In all the confusion I forgot to tell you our grandchildren were coming. Thank you, though."

"Grandpa, are you all right?"

"How'd the fire start?"

"Are the horses hurt?"

"Where's Gram?"

"I'm right here, dearies. Stand back, this is hot." Their grandmother came from behind the oven, carrying a pan of cornbread with a mitt on each hand. She set it on the long oak table that filled the center of the kitchen.

Eight men and women in yellow pants with red suspenders ate hungrily as Grandpa ladled chili into their bowls.

"We're so glad you kids are okay," said Del Bridger. She introduced them to the firefighters whose names they had learned as soon as they stepped into the house. "We've been out of sorts all day worrying about you, heartsick about the fire. But look at you three! Taller and so grown up since the last time you were here, my word."

"Gram, that was just a few months ago," Claire laughed. She threw herself into the woman's arms and breathed in the warm smell of supper. "Are the horses okay? The barns are all burned up."

"And did someone die?" David asked. "The bus driver said there was a terrible incident."

Mr. Bridger put a strong arm around the boys. He was tall and lean with the rugged good-looks of a cowboy. He wore boots, jeans, and a western shirt with snap pockets. He said, "Remember Riley our ranch hand?"

"Yep," said David. "He taught us how to rope a calf."

"And he let us ride his appaloosa." Claire pronounced this carefully.

"Grandpa, what happened?" Jeff wanted to know. "Is Riley okay?"

The man crossed his arms and leaned against the refrigerator. He so resembled the boys' dad—Russell Bridger, who had died last winter in an avalanche—that the cousins felt comforted being with their grandfather.

"I'm not proud of this," he began, "but this morning Riley and I exchanged hot words. Things have been missing from around here like Gram's iPhone. When Riley suddenly had extra money to buy a new saddle, well, we wondered."

"Did you accuse him of stealing?" Jeff asked. His brown eyes were serious.

"Nossir," said Grandpa. He filled his pipe with fresh tobacco from a pouch in his pocket. He tamped it down with his thumb. "I just asked about things and Riley stormed out. He's a grown man, but he was too upset to talk. An hour later when Gram and I were making a pot of coffee we saw flames—"

"I bet Riley started the fire!" David shouted, pulling his sketchbook from his pack. He drew the ranch hand smoking a cigarette.

Grandpa struck a stick match against the table to light his pipe. "Hold on a moment boy," he said. "We're not going to jump to conclusions here. Riley is an old family friend—"

"What about the horses?" Claire interrupted.

"They escaped, honey. Broke down the gate of the paddock when they smelled smoke."

"Oh, good!" she cried.

Jeff sighed a big breath. "Whew! I was worried about them, especially the ponies you keep for us to ride."

"Me, too," said the younger boy.

14

"By now," Grandpa continued, "they're on the far reaches of this ranch, maybe up in one of the canyons. We'll start looking first thing tomorrow."

"We can find them, right?" Claire formed her hands into a prayer.

"Sure hope so. There've been rustlers though, sneaking onto some of the ranches around here. Thieves in the middle of the night."

"Maybe Riley knows them," David said.

Jeff put his hand on his brother's arm to keep him quiet. "Did anyone have to go to the hospital? We saw an ambulance."

Grandpa replied, "No one from here. The crew got another call from up the road. Mr. Winchester fell off his ladder and broke his ankle."

"All right dearies, time to sit down and eat." Del Bridger wore jeans and boots like her husband, and a plaid western shirt. As usual, her gray hair was in a braid down her back. But today there were wisps around her face, making her look tired. "My word, nine o'clock already. It's been a long day for everyone. A devastating day."

She took a bowl from the fridge. "Do you kids still like fresh strawberries with whipped cream on top?"

"*Gram,*" they said together, grinning at her familiar question.

She winked at them. "Well, I'm just making sure. Thanks happen to change a person's mind."

3
The Bunkhouse

*G*ram flicked on a lamp in the bunkhouse then opened a cupboard. "Your sleeping bags are in here from last time, and extra blankets in case a storm comes up. The skylights are open to cool off the room, but if it starts raining you know what to do."

Claire hugged her grandmother. "Thanks, Gram. But maybe Buddy should be out here with us."

"We don't need a guard dog," said Jeff.

"Yeah Claire," his brother agreed. "This isn't called Lucky Bridger Ranch for nothing."

"True," Gram said. "We've never had to lock our doors. But just the same, please latch up when I leave. Now try to get some sleep. You know when breakfast is, right?"

"Sunrise!" the three answered.

"See you tomorrow then." She blew them a kiss, closing the door behind her.

Claire jumped up to lock the deadbolt. Then she and the boys unrolled their bedding and picked their usual spots. The bunkhouse was a small log cabin that had been the original homestead from when the Bridgers settled there in the 1800s.

Grandpa had modernized it by installing electricity and a bathroom. When the roof leaked he repaired it with skylights so his grandchildren would be able to see the stars at night. On either side of the stone fireplace he built bookshelves then added his final touch: a cozy chair at each window with a reading lamp.

"This'll be good for you," he often told them. But they didn't share his enthusiasm.

"I wish Grandpa would let us have TV," said Jeff. "Like Riley's bunk house."

"Me, too," David agreed.

Claire said, "Well, I'm going to get organized. Dibs on the dresser."

"You can have it." David unzipped his pack and shook it until his clothes fell in a wrinkled pile, which he left on the floor. Jeff did the same, but he draped his shirts over the back of a chair.

17

Next, the boys kicked off their sneakers and abandoned them where they landed, in the center of the room.

They admired their mess, giving each other a fist bump. "Just like home," Jeff smiled.

"I think we should plan for our day tomorrow," Claire suggested. She went to each window and closed the checkered curtains. They were new and crisply starched. She put her clock on the nightstand by her bed. "I'll set the alarm for five."

The brothers stared at her. *"Five?"* they said.

"Yeah, so we don't miss breakfast."

"Whatever you say, Miss Bossy." David said this as he flung his socks into the air.

"So," she continued, "we have to help Gram and Grandpa solve who started the fire. And who took their things? It used to feel safe out here, but now it's all weird."

Claire untied her hiking boots and placed them neatly under her bed, with a sock in each one. When she bent down to line them up she peered under the mattress.

"Hey, look at this." She dropped to her belly to wiggle underneath then wiggled backward holding a cardboard tube the length of a ruler.

"What's that?" Jeff asked.

Claire shook the tube. It rustled with something inside.

"I use these at school for my paintings." David uncapped its plastic end. Out slipped a rolled-up canvas. It crackled as if quite old. Together they spread it on the plank floor, holding down the corners to keep it flat.

"Is this a map?" Claire wondered.

The cousins stared at a drawing with squiggles and lines. The edges were frayed. Some of the markings were smudged, making it hard to read, but soon they realized it was indeed a map. It showed a stream running into a large pond and several canyons. Elegant penmanship spelled *Hidden Horse Ranch* with the date *1882*. A log cabin and outhouse were the only buildings on what appeared to be a vast acreage.

"Wow, this is from the olden days," said Claire.

Jeff pointed to Box Canyon. "Remember Grandpa told us about stagecoach robbers? How they hid here with the horses then sneaked 'em away by moonlight? It sorta looks like a shoebox with cliffs on three sides."

"The canyon is a dead end, that's for sure," said David. His blue eyes were merry. He loved telling this story. "And the bad guys dragged brush across the opening for camouflage."

"Yep. Hidden Horse Ranch," Claire said. "I like how this place got its official name. It's mysterious." She looked under her bed again. "Guys, is there a flashlight handy?"

David rummaged through his pile of clothes. "Right here."

19

Claire kneeled and aimed the light in a dark corner. An object sparkled. She crawled underneath again, but this time brought out a silver pen. She looked at it closely then handed it to Jeff.

 He whistled through his teeth. "Wow, this was Dad's! See, his name is engraved: *Russell Bridger*. How'd it get out here?"

"It looks valuable, so does the map," said Claire.

David spoke in a quiet voice, glancing at the door. "What if Riley stole them to sell at an antique store? He lives in the other bunkhouse, so no one would suspect he'd come in here—"

"But he and Dad were friends ever since they were little," said Jeff. "Why would he … shhh. What's that noise?"

The cousins froze. Above the sound of crickets they heard footsteps outside. Someone walked slowly around the cabin, pausing at each window.

"Who could it be?" whispered Claire. "It's the middle of the night."

Jeff put his finger to his lips so no one would speak then motioned for David to help him. The brothers tiptoed to the card table. Carefully and quietly they carried one of the stiff chairs over to the doorknob and wedged it under the latch. Someone trying to break the lock would not have an easy time getting inside.

20

The cousins listened. They waited for the footsteps to go away, but instead there was a new sound: a swish against the door as if someone had leaned against it.

4
Keeping Watch

The cousins stared at the door. Finally Claire whispered, "I'm starting to freak out."

"Me, too. Should we should yell for Grandpa?" asked David.

"Uh, maybe we should wait," said Jeff. "If Grandpa thinks we're babies, he'll make us sleep in the house. And that would be a total bummer."

"Oh, right. So what should we do?" David's whisper was loud.

"Let's call him on our walkie-talkies," Claire said, "just to say goodnight. Then later if we need to scream bloody murder he'll hear us."

"Good idea." Jeff pulled his two-way radio from under his pillow and clicked the switch.

"Good evening, Grandfather. This is Jeff. We're turning in now. See you tomorrow. Over." A crackling came through his speaker. "Grandpa, hello? Do you read? Over."

Silence.

"Maybe he's brushing his teeth," Claire suggested. "Wait. Do you hear that?"

From the corner where David had thrown his pack came a muffled crackling. He said, "Uh … I left Cheetos in the pocket. *Something* is eating them."

The cousins listened. After a moment Claire marched to the corner and reached into David's backpack. She pulled out his walkie-talkie and held it up.

"Jeff Bridger," she said, "that noise was *you* calling David who's right here. We forgot to leave one of these in the house. Now what?"

In response, David grabbed his flashlight and lay on his stomach. He turned his head sideways to look through the space below the bottom of the door.

"Weird," he whispered. "The welcome mat is all bunched up like a furry rug. It's blocking the light from Gram's porch."

Claire said, "I knew it. Someone's trying to trap us in here. What if they have a match—"

"Wait a second." Jeff got on his belly to look. "We need something pointy."

Claire rushed to the fireplace. A stuffed rainbow trout was mounted over the mantel with a fishing rod. She lifted the pole from its rack and handed it to Jeff. Now all three were lying on the floor straining to see what was outside, their flashlights making shadowy bumps.

Gently Jeff pushed the pole through the gap and tapped the rug.

The rug moved. Then it made a sniffing sound.

"A wolf!" David said. "I can tell by its fur."

"Dude, a wolf wouldn't just sit on the doorstep. They're wild and they run around. Maybe it's Buddy." Jeff let go of the rod to see what would happen.

To their surprise it jiggled, as if someone were pulling it from outside.

"Wolves don't like sticks," David declared.

"How do you know? You're just making that up," said Jeff.

"Well, he's probably hungry," David insisted, "and he smelled fish on the end of the rod."

"Yoo-hoo, guys?" Claire called to them from a window, which she had opened. "It's not a wolf. And it's not Buddy."

"What is it?" the brothers asked.

"Watch this." She pulled the chair away from the door then opened it. "Hello there. What're you doing here, Reesha?"

A medium-sized dog looked up at the cousins, wagging a stump of a tail. Its mouth pulled back as if smiling.

"How do you know his name?" asked Jeff.

Claire bent down. She touched the pink, heart-shaped tag dangling from the dog's collar. "Right here. It's says Reesha. And she's a girl, not a boy."

"Where's her owner?" David wondered. "And why isn't Buddy here patrolling? Maybe Reesha is lost." He offered her a cookie from his lunch but Claire snatched it away.

"Chocolate is poison to dogs!" she cried. "Here, give her some little crackers. Mom baked them with veggies so they're healthy. I brought a whole bag."

Jeff patted his knee to invite her in. "Here girl, you can stay with us."

"She looks like a cattle dog," said David, "a red heeler. My teacher brought hers to class before school ended. They're real loyal and smart."

25

The cousins sat on the floor, petting and talking to their new friend. They gave her a bowl of water. Claire brought a blanket from the cupboard and made a cozy bed by the door. When she patted it, Reesha stepped onto the soft fabric. With her front paws she dug up a little nest then curled into it.

Claire slipped into her sleeping bag and pulled it up to her chin for warmth. With her foot she felt for the pajamas that she'd stored there earlier. Then she wiggled out of her clothes and rolled them into balls to keep at her feet. "Guys, it's like Reesha's guarding us or something."

"Mm-huh," the brothers mumbled. They had gone to bed with their clothes on.

"I'm glad we'll be here for a few weeks," she chattered on. "We can help Gram and Grandpa then we'll all feel safe again. Oh, aren't these stars beautiful?" Claire tried to keep watching the sky, but her eyes were heavy. It was nearly midnight.

Just once more though, she wanted to check on the stray dog. She tiptoed across the cold floor. Reesha was still curled on the blanket. One ear twitched.

"Good-night little cattle dog," she said softly.

Now all was quiet in the bunkhouse. Stars blinked and shimmered overhead and a breeze came in through the skylights.

The cabin was dark except for two beams of light shining against the wall. Already Jeff and David were sound asleep. Before returning to her bed, Claire crept to their bunks and turned off their flashlights.

"So your batteries don't run down," she whispered.

5
Cold Pancakes

*C*laire bolted awake and looked at her clock. Morning sunlight filled the cabin.

"Jeff, David, it's eight-thirty! We slept through the alarm."

The brothers groaned from their bunks while Claire dressed inside her sleeping bag. Her clothes were nice and warm from being beside her all night.

"Guys, maybe Grandpa knows who Reesha belongs to. Let's hurry and not forget our backpacks."

Jeff put on a clean T-shirt then rummaged in the pile for his shoes. His brown hair was short and didn't need a comb, but David's was wild and yellow as a haystack. His shirt was still inside out from yesterday.

The brothers caught up to Claire at the burned stables. The odor of charred wood stung the air. Strips of yellow tape formed a barrier, with signs: CRIME SCENE! DANGER! KEEP OUT!

 "I'm so glad the horses weren't here when the fire started," Claire said in a quiet voice.

"Me, too," said David.

"It would've been a catastrophe," Jeff explained. "Gram told me their instinct is to stay in their safe place, even if it's burning. The horses would have died."

*T*he aroma of roasted almonds greeted the cousins when they neared the ranch house.

"'Morning, Gram!" they called, trooping into the kitchen with Reesha.

No one answered. They noticed dishes drying on the counter and the empty skillet on the stove. The table had been wiped clean. A note was propped against the jug of matches Grandpa used for lighting his pipe:

Good morning, dearies.

Grandpa and I are with neighbors rounding up the herd by jeep, we hope—borrowed saddles, etc. so we can ride home. Buddy came, too. Help yourselves to leftovers. Love, Gram

29

The cousins exchanged looks of disappointment. "Gram sure runs a tight ship," David lamented.

"Well, we *are* a few hours late," said Claire.

"So now what? I'm starved," Jeff said.

Claire searched the fridge. She took out a blue platter covered with foil. It was heavy with oat pancakes. She set it on the table with jars of Gram's homemade jam and almond butter. In the cupboard she found baking supplies.

"Ta-da! We can make sandwiches with raisins and cinnamon red-hots."

"That's more like it," said David.

Jeff filled three glasses of water at the sink then sat down. "Time to call a meeting," he said.

"Good idea," Claire agreed. "We need to study all the clues."

David took a bite of pancake oozing jam then opened his sketchbook. With his free hand he made two columns. Under LOST, he drew several items: a cell phone, a horse, and the burned down stables. Under FOUND, he sketched a squiggly map and the pen.

"Hmm," he said with a loud swallow, "none of these connect to anything."

"Not yet," said Jeff.

"Hello? Hello?" came a woman's voice from a far bedroom. Clippy-clop steps came through the house to the kitchen.

30

"I'm dearly happy to see you angels. When you arrived last night, I was out at a movie. It's dreadful about the fire, just dreadful."

"Hi there, Aunt Alice!" Claire jumped up to hug Gram's twin. The elderly sisters were identical except for their clothes. Aunt Alice wore a Sunday dress with a string of pearls around her neck. The black purse on her arm matched her sturdy shoes. She called the cousins various words that meant 'angels' because she kept forgetting their names.

"Did you cherubs find my silk scarf?" she asked, squishing the brothers into a hug. She smelled good, like vanilla and almonds from her favorite lotion. "It's blue," she said. "I left it in the bunkhouse the other day when I was hanging new curtains for your grandmother."

"Uh, we didn't see a scarf." Claire glanced at the boys.

"Dear me. So you found nothing?"

"Well we did find—" David began, but Jeff interrupted.

"Aunt Alice, did you ask Gram about it?"

"Yes dear. She was out riding so I called her cell phone several times. A strange man answered. He had no idea what I was talking about."

"A strange man?" Claire asked.

"I'm afraid so, my angels. Well now, I'm going to make myself a nice cup of tea. If you want to chat, I'll be on the front porch with my knitting." She set the kettle on the stove.

31

While waiting for the water to boil, Aunt Alice looked through the cupboards.

The cousins whispered to one another.

"Why didn't you ask her about the map and pen?" David asked his older brother.

"Because I didn't want her to think we were accusing her. If she ran away like Riley did, Gram would be heartbroken."

Claire nodded slowly. "That's a really good point. Shh ... now what is she doing?"

Aunt Alice opened the wide mouth of her purse and dropped in a can of tuna. A jar of olives held her interest as she read the label then she added that, too. Her purse snapped shut with a loud click.

"She lives here with Gram and Grandpa, so why is she swiping things?" David whispered.

Jeff said, "Remember last time? When she came away from the hall closet, her purse was so stuffed, it wouldn't close."

"Something fishy's going on." David returned to his sketchbook. In a new column marked SUSPECTS he wrote, *Aunt Alice* then *missing scarf.* He tapped his pencil on the table, thinking and thinking.

Finally he sketched Riley in his cowboy hat. He drew a line to the missing phone and added, "*Strange man who answered.*"

Then on a new page he drew Riley carrying a small child in his arms. Both were dripping wet. He said, "Jeff, remember when I was little and I fell into the river?"

"You got caught under a log," answered his brother. "You were drowning, but Riley rescued you."

David sighed. "Yep. I wonder where he is right now."

6
Clues

After breakfast, the cousins went into Grandpa's study. They put the pen and cardboard tube on his desk then gazed out his picture window. The view was beautiful. Acres of pastures and distant hills framed the ranch, the sky was tall and blue. A creek meandered through a grove of oak trees, feeding fresh, cold water into a pond.

"You guys up for a swim?" asked David. It was going to be another hot day.

"Definitely," Jeff said. "Maybe first we can help Grandpa at the barns, what's left of them, raking up ashes or something. He likes it when we do stuff without having to ask."

"On it!" cried David. "And if Riley left clues, we'll find 'em."

"Let's surprise Gram by cleaning up," Claire said, leading them into the kitchen. They rinsed their plates in the sink then hurried out to the stables.

*T*he sun was rising into a bright blue sky. The cousins were surprised to see a man with a clipboard inside the police tape. His black polo shirt and ball cap had emblems from the fire department. A lanyard hung from his neck with his photo I.D.

"Hello, Inspector Luna," Jeff read from the nametag. "Anything we can help you with?"

"No thanks, kid. I'm about done here."

"We're wondering how the fire started," said David. "We have our suspicions."

"Is that so? At first it appeared to be arson."

"Arson? You mean, someone started it for a bad reason?" Claire asked.

"That's the general idea. Yes."

Jeff was glad his shirt was tucked in like the inspector's. It made him feel important. "Sir, how can you tell?" he asked.

The man clicked his pen then wrote on his clipboard. "We look for hot spots, to see where it began. But in this case, I didn't find any cans of gasoline. No cigarettes or matches either."

"Oh." David sounded disappointed. "We thought Riley caused it. He smokes cigarettes."

"Doubtful, young man. It's probably some sort of spontaneous combustion. A phantom, so to speak."

"What! A phantom?" cried Jeff.

"Meaning, the fire may have started by itself. Anything else?" The man glanced up at the sun. "It's too hot to stand around chit-chatting, so make it quick."

One by one the cousins shrugged. They were still full of questions but not sure what to ask.

"All right then. I'll submit my report to the fire chief. Then I'll come back tomorrow with a copy for your grandparents." As the inspector gathered his tools to leave, the kids peered over the yellow tape.

"There must be a clue somewhere," said Jeff.

"Hey, what's that?" David pointed to a spec of white among the burned wood. When he did, Reesha trotted into the ashes to retrieve it.

"Come back, girl!" Claire cried. "You'll get hurt."

But Reesha pawed through the ashes and returned to the children with what looked like a bone. She dropped it at their feet.

"What is *this*?" Jeff picked up the remains of a large magnifying glass. The handle was about eight inches long and charred with soot. The round metal frame that would have held a lens—for it was missing—was the size of a small plate.

36

He wiped it against his jeans then gave it to his brother. "Didn't Grandpa have one like this?"

"I think so. For reading tiny things up close."

"Like an old map," Claire said with satisfaction.

"Exactly," said Jeff. "But what's it doing out here?"

"And why didn't the handle melt? It's plastic," David observed.

"Good question. Hey dude, remember when we used one of these on Lost Island?"

"Ooh yeah," said David. "That was rad. We were trying to burn an ant hill, but instead caught a bush on fire."

Claire crossed her arms. "*Hello?* Lucky we were on the lake and someone like *me* had a big bucket for water."

Jeff gave her ponytail an affectionate yank. "If it wasn't for you Miss Bossy, we would've burned down the fort, too. Talk about a close call."

"Okay," David went on, "what if Riley stole this? When he got mad at Grandpa he used it to spark the hay."

"Awesome clue," said Jeff. "Sir?"

The inspector was using his elbow to roll up the yellow tape. "What is it, young man?"

"Mr. Luna, could a lens have started this fire?"

"Certainly, but it would've taken time, and the sun would have had to be shining at a precise angle into the stall." The man adjusted his ball cap then shook his head.

37

"Honestly, I've studied fires for years and have never known an arsonist to be that patient. Sometimes weird things happen that can't be explained. I'm taking off now. There's broken glass and nails so you kids be careful."

After the inspector drove away in his pickup, the cousins continued to look around. They searched for remains to a cell phone then turned their attention to the blackened magnifier. When they noticed marks on the handle, Jeff said, "Doesn't this look like something chewed on it?"

"Totally," the younger boy agreed.

"Sure does," said Claire.

They went over to Reesha who had settled in the shade of a tree. Jeff showed it to her. "Did you do this, girl?" His voice was gentle, but the cattle dog lowered her head and turned away. Her ears lay back as if she'd been scolded.

"Aw, poor girl," said Claire. "She's either guilty or really sensitive."

"Tess and Rascal would do the same," said Jeff. "Especially Yum-Yum." He was referring to their dogs at home in Cabin Creek.

David said, "Well, it's kinda suspicious, if you ask me."

A tiny plume of dust rose in the distance. The cousins shaded their eyes with their hands and saw small moving shapes. "I think those are horses!" Claire cried.

As they watched the herd come their way, Jeff had an idea. "Guys, I know who we can interview next."

7
The Interview

*G*randpa rode up on his gray gelding, dust clouding around him as he reined to a stop. A rope around the horn of his saddle was tied to a pony that loped behind him. He waved his hat to the children when he saw them perched on a log fence.

Two others on horseback followed, each leading a runaway into the corral. Gram soon trotted up on her Morgan, which was chestnut-colored. Her braid bounced against her back as she stood in her stirrups.

"Found these five in Box Canyon," she called to her grandchildren. She slid out of her saddle and came over to them. Her jeans and red cowboy boots were dusty from her ride. "We're still missing our mare. Her colt ran away, too."

"Oh no!" Claire cried. "She has a baby and it's lost?"

"Yes dear, but don't worry. Aunt Alice is making lunch so we can hurry out again after we eat."

Grandpa put a hand on Jeff's shoulder. "You alright, boy? You look upset."

"We're glad most of the horses are back," he answered. "But where's Buddy? We need to ask him something, I mean we want to see him."

"He'll be here soon," Grandpa laughed. "That Rottweiler is funny. He'd rather hang around the stables and watch the world go by. He's friends with all the horses, but he can't run and run like little cattle dogs."

"You mean like this one?" Claire pointed to Reesha.

"Yes honey. I see you've met our new family member. Come here, girl." He patted his hip then took out a biscuit. "She knows I keep a treat in my pocket."

Reesha came to Mr. Bridger, sat, and looked up at him. She lifted her front paw as if to say, *"please?"*

"We didn't know you got a new dog, Grandpa," said David.

"Well, we weren't planning on it. But we found her a couple weeks ago down by the pond getting a drink. She was starved and her fur was caked with mud."

"Is she lost?" Jeff asked.

"We think so," said Gram. "We put up ads, made calls, but no one has claimed her yet. Best we can tell, Reesha fell from the bed of a pickup."

"Poor thing," Claire.

"It's sad, but it happens," Gram went on. "A wrangler passes through town. He takes a corner too fast, keeps driving, but doesn't know his poor dog tumbled out."

Grandpa said, "Her instinct is to herd. Makes us laugh the way she keeps Buddy close to the house. Say, what's that you've got there, David?" He reached for the broken magnifying glass. "Well I'll be. Find this in the ashes, did you?"

"Yes, is it yours?"

 Grandpa examined the handle. "Sure looks like it, minus these teeth marks. Mine went missing a few months ago. Well, look who's here for lunch."

With his hat he gestured to the dirt road bordering the pastures. Dust spun in a cloud as a jeep pulled into sight. A dark figure sat beside the driver, staring straight ahead.

"Who is that?"

"Best co-pilot I ever saw. Doesn't take his eyes off the road." Grandpa laughed again. When the jeep parked near the corral the driver opened the door and out jumped Buddy.

"Here boy, fetch!" Jeff threw a stick across the yard. Buddy loped over to where it landed, gave it a long sniff, but returned to the children without it. Meanwhile, Reesha raced to the stick and circled back, dropping it at Jeff's feet.

Claire and the brothers took turns tossing more sticks. Each time, Buddy sniffed, but that was it. Only the cattle dog liked retrieving.

Jeff threw his hands up. "Well! Maybe Reesha's the thief. It's sure not Buddy or Riley."

Mr. Bridger gazed at the row of burned stables. "Riley and your dad built these stalls when they were teenagers. It hurts something terrible to think—" His voice trailed off.

"Grandfather," said David, wanting to console him, "we'll help you make new ones. Even though I'm not as big as Jeff, I can carry lumber and we're good with the hammer, so is Claire. Don't worry."

The man looked at the boys with fondness. "You're more like your dad every day. He'd be so proud of you both. I'm thankful you found his pen. We gave it to him for graduating high school."

As they walked to the ranch house for lunch, the cousins described the fire inspector. When they mentioned finding the map, their grandparents gave each other a puzzled look.

"That's odd," said Grandpa. He removed his hat to fan his face. "It disappeared last Christmas. We didn't report it stolen because we thought maybe it got mixed up with the tubes of wrapping paper we threw out and—" Again, his voice grew soft.

"Children," Gram continued for him, "at that time there was a lot of commotion. Even though the map was quite valuable, we were worried about other things as you can imagine."

She put her arm around Jeff and David. They knew she was thinking about their father and that terrible day of the avalanche.

They walked on in silence. When they reached the kitchen door Claire turned to the brothers. "Hey! Reesha couldn't have stolen the map and pen because she wasn't here at Christmas—"

"*Yeah,*" said David, "and since this Rottweiler doesn't fetch, that leaves Riley as a suspect."

"And," Jeff said in a whisper, "Aunt Alice."

8
The Invisible Rope

After lunch the cousins hiked to the pond in their swimming suits, towels over their shoulders. It was hot and they were eager to jump in the cool water. It took ten minutes from the bunkhouse, along a trail scratchy with sagebrush. Reesha supervised by trotting beside them.

Earlier in June the kids had passed a Junior Lifesaving course at the Blue Mountain Marina. Now that Jeff was twelve they were allowed to swim in this protected pond without adults. But today Grandpa met them there with a surprise: an old rubber tire that he had hauled in his pick-up.

Jeff and Claire hurried to climb one of the oak trees that shaded the bank. It was nearly two hundred years old, its limbs thick with age. "Ready!" they called down to their grandfather.

A coil of rope flew up to them. They caught it then wrapped it around the branch. Jeff tied a sturdy knot as his dad had taught him. "Ready," he said again.

David waited below. He steadied the dangling rope while Grandpa attached the tire. It hung like a pendulum several inches off the ground.

"Thanks, Grandpa!" David cried. He grabbed the tire and with a running push, swung out wide over the water then let go. Arms around his knees, he cannonballed into a terrific splash. He bubbled to the surface, hair in his eyes, swimming madly for shore.

"Yowee, it's freeeezing!" he cried. Even in summer, the water was cold from snow melting in the mountains. Reesha paddled out to David, staying beside him until he reached the shallows.

Jeff started down the tree to join him, but Claire climbed up instead. She was curious about some markings she'd noticed on the higher branches. "You won't believe what's up here," she shouted. "Someone carved their name a jillion years ago. Grandpa, come look."

"Just tell me what it says, honey. Hold on tight. I don't want you to fall."

"I'm being careful, Grandpa." She scooted around the tree, using the limbs as steps. Claire had practiced this all summer in their Lookout Tower on Lost Island. "The letters are too faded to read, but there's a date. Looks like 1882. Wonder who did this?"

"Kids from the olden days," Jeff yelled as he stepped onto the swing. He launched himself into the pond. After the splash and resulting wave, he came up for air. "Claire, your turn. It's epic!"

"In a minute. Grandpa, what happened in 1882?"

"Let me think. Well, our great uncles and so forth came west on the Oregon Trail before then. They homesteaded right here, and became mountain men and fur trappers."

"But was there a murder or something?" she asked.

"Hm. As I recall, yes. There's a story about horse thieves and a shoot-out in 1882."

"I remember that date!" she said. "It's on your old map, the one we found in the bunkhouse. It's a clue."

"A clue to what?" asked David. He crawled out of the water and stood dripping on the muddy bank with Reesha.

Grandpa went to his truck, which was parked in the shade. His pipe was on the dashboard, unlit. Because of the fire hazard, he never smoked around brush. He uncapped the cardboard tube then spread the map on the front seat. With the pipe stem he pointed to the date. "You're right, honey. It does say 1882."

"Guys, there's something else up here."

"What it is, Claire?" Jeff yelled up to her.

"Well, it's hard to see because bark has grown over it. It circles the branch like a big fat rope, except it feels smooth like a scar. I bet as the tree grew, the rope rotted."

47

"*Rope?*" said Jeff. His knee was on the tire swing, ready to push off. He hesitated. "You sure?"

"Yeah, I'm touching it," she said, "or at least the scar it left behind."

"I knew it!" cried the younger boy.

"Knew what?" Jeff said.

"This was a hanging tree for horse thieves." David shouted so loud, sparrows on the branch overhead rose up in noisy flight.

"Dude, that's just a wild guess."

"Maybe, maybe not," said Grandpa. He used the stem of his pipe to trace the squiggles of the map. He squinted and squinted. Finally he took a pair of reading glasses from the glove compartment. "Blast! Can hardly see anymore. Gram made me get these things so I could read. Now boys, look at this with me. I've puzzled over this riddle for years."

The brothers dried themselves off then leaned into the cab of the truck. Jeff read the tiny words: '*Where dead boots point, there hide the coins.*' Grandpa, this sounds like a poem. What's it mean?"

48

Claire scurried down the tree. She pushed the tire so it swung gently. "I think I know. If a bad guy got hung here—" she looked up through the tall branches— "then his boots would've pointed"—she stomped her foot on the ground—"right here."

"I think two things happened," said Jeff.

"Me, too!" David agreed. "A robber or horse thief got hung—"

Jeff finished his brother's sentence, "*Then* someone buried coins here. The dude planned to come back for them—"

"*But*," Claire chimed in, "he needed to escape and only had time to draw this map with a clue."

Their grandfather smiled. "I surely do enjoy you three. Boys, when your dad was young we searched with shovels all over this ranch and pond. For years we explored."

"Did you find any bodies?" David asked with enthusiasm.

Grandpa put his arm around David. "Sorry Grandson, but all we found were rusted wagon parts and horseshoes. Once an old fiddle in an old box, but that's it. No treasure, no bodies."

Jeff's brows furrowed in thought. "Okay. But whoever took the map, probably thinks there's still buried gold. They lit the fire to draw attention away from this pond."

"But no one's been digging here," David said. "See, how the ground is smooth?"

"Hey guys," said Claire. "Even if the thief knew the riddle was about a tree, there're trees all over the place. How would he know to climb *this* one, then discover the old rope scar, then figure out to dig *here*?" Again she stomped her foot to mark the spot.

"All good questions," Grandpa replied. He sat on the open tailgate of his truck, gazing up at the branches. Leaves rustled from a pair of chipmunks chasing each other. From the surrounding sagebrush came the clicking of cicadas, loud in the afternoon heat.

Moments passed. Then Claire said, "Grandpa, did the map get stolen out of your safe?"

"Nope. It was on my desk because I finally decided to frame it. Call me a dreamer, but I love the history of this place and I like thinking there still could be gold coins hidden around here."

"Wait. A. Second," said Jeff. "Grandpa, who did you tell about this, I mean the map maybe having clues?"

Mr. Bridger pushed his hat off his head to wipe his brow. "Gram, of course. And since she tells her sister everything, Aunt Alice probably knows, too. Also Riley. Every week I leave his paycheck on my desk. He's always been curious about the treasure."

Claire smiled. "Ah-ha! Two of our suspects connect to the map. David, get your sketchbook."

"Okay, Miss Bossy, but first things first." He handed the tire swing to her so she would climb on. Then he and Jeff pushed it as high as it would go. She flew through the air and tucked into a cannonball.

"Yabbadabbadoooo!" she yelled before soaking her cousins with an expert splash.

9

Accomplices

*G*randpa rolled up the map then
pulled his cell phone from his
pocket to check the time. "Gotta
go. Gram and I are riding out
again. Hope to find the mare
and her colt before sunset. You
kids have fun now and be safe."
From the back of his truck he
took out a small cooler.

"Treats! Thanks, Grandpa."

"Well, thank your grandmother. She knows that
swimming makes you hungry."

David opened the lid. "My favorite, salami and
rice crackers!"

"Mine, too," said Mr. Bridger.

"Grandpa?" Claire said. "What if someone tries to
burn down the bunkhouse while we're sleeping? Or
your house? We could all die."

"Oh honey, try not to worry. The smoke detectors
have fresh batteries. Also, the police will be patrolling
our road. They don't want anything to happen either."

"Whew, that's a relief," said Jeff. "Grandpa, before you go, I have another question."

"Yes, boy?"

"I'm curious when you last saw Gram's iPhone. In your study?"

He squinted at the sky, thinking. "Let's see. Last Sunday. I was on the porch reading. Gram brought me a snack, and also her cell. Even though reception out here is iffy, she wanted me to program a new ring-tone."

David took out his sketchpad. "By chance, did Riley see you there?" he asked. He quickly drew Grandpa on the porch with closed eyes. For fun he added a bubble over his head with ZZZs to show that his grandfather had fallen asleep.

"Hm," said Grandpa. "Yes, matter of fact Riley was with me. We often sit there together after church to enjoy the view of the mountains. This good little cattle dog was there, too." He bent down to pet Reesha.

Claire leaned into Grandpa's arm to hug him. "Then did you have a snooze like usual, Grandfather?"

He laughed. "No honey. I went into the house because Aunt Alice needed help with the TV remote."

"Were you away from the porch a long time?" asked Jeff.

"Maybe ten minutes. When I came outside, Riley was gone. And so was the cellphone." Grandpa laughed again. "You kids sound like FBI agents."

The cousins grinned at one another. Jeff said, "I bet Reesha chased him away when she saw him take your stuff."

"I don't think so. She was still sitting by my chair, waiting."

David said, "Then it looks like Riley is guilty."

"Sure seems that way," said Grandpa. "But I want to hear his side of the story. By the way, it was his idea to build this rope swing."

"It was?"

"Yessir. He wanted you kids to have extra fun this summer. Now I really must go."

He patted his belt where his walkie-talkie was clipped. "I've got this turned to your frequency, so call if you need us. Some day there'll be satellite towers out here and I'll get you detectives a cellphone. Meanwhile, see you tonight at supper."

After Grandpa drove away, the cousins spread their towels on a grassy bank.

"Time for another meeting," Claire announced. She was breathless with a new theory. "Aunt Alice and Riley are accomplices! She made a fuss with the TV so that he could grab the loot from the porch when Grandpa came inside."

"That must be it!" said David. In the SUSPECTS column he circled Riley and Aunt Alice with an arrow pointing to the phone in the LOST column.

From the cooler, Jeff took out the box of crackers. He ate a handful while watching his brother draw. "Okay," he said, "but what about the fire? Did Aunt Alice start it then hide the match so the investigator wouldn't see it?"

"No way," said Claire. "She's kinda goofy, but she wouldn't do anything to harm Gram. Do you think she has Alzheimer's?"

"I've been wondering about that," Jeff said. "It's weird her scarf vanished though."

David put his pencil behind his ear. "Yeah, weird all right. Like a phantom took it. So now what?"

"Well, one thing for sure," said Jeff. "Our grandparents need us. The sooner we solve who started the fire—"

"The sooner we'll all feel safe again!" Claire cried.

"So," Jeff continued, "We've got to find the thief before more stuff disappears. Gram and Grandpa shouldn't have to worry about this. Especially on top of the missing horses and having to build new stables."

Claire combed her hands through her drying hair. She shook out the curls and made a ponytail from the elastic around her wrist. Then she burst into a laugh. "Guys, isn't it awesome how he called us 'detectives'?"

"Totally," said David.
Jeff gave a thumbs-up.
"So let's keep thinking."

10
A Strange Voice

 *I*n the shade of the oak tree, the kids shared the crackers. They gazed out at the pond. Its surface quivered with mosquitos. A speckled trout jumped, causing ripples to spread to the bank. David glanced at the dangling tire then began sketching.

"Why are you drawing the tire swing?" Claire wanted to know.

"It gives me a nice thought about Riley," David answered. "He wanted to build this for us, but something bizarre-o happened. The barns burned and now he's missing."

"The swing is another clue," Jeff said. "We have to keep an eye on this place. If someone starts digging out here, we'll know it's the person who stole the map."

The cousins fell quiet with their thoughts. As the sun moved overhead, the dappled shade grew hot. Already their bathing suits had dried from their swim.

Finally Claire jumped up and ran into the pond. "I'm roasting!" she cried.

"Me, too!" David somersaulted into the water then swam out to her. They splashed each other with big kicks, yelling for Jeff to join them.

But Jeff was staring at his backpack. A man's voice came from his walkie-talkie. He took it out to answer, quickly fumbling with the switch.

"Hi Grandpa. This is Jeff. Over."

"…anyone there…hello?" said the voice.

"Did you find the horses, Grandpa? Over." There was no reply, so he turned up the volume. It crackled and hissed.

"Hello?" Jeff repeated.

When David and Claire saw the older boy waving frantically for them to get out of the water, they swam to shore. They stood dripping beside him.

"What's the matter?" asked Claire. "What did Grandpa say?"

"Are we in trouble?" David worried.

Jeff held the two-way radio at arm's length, turning it for a better reception. He clicked the on-off button several times. With a look of concern, he said, "That didn't sound like Grandpa."

"Maybe it was one of the neighbors who is helping," Claire suggested.

58

"Uh, I don't think so. I'm pretty sure it was Riley."

"*Riley?*" David yelled. "How did he get Grandpa's walkie-talkie?"

Jeff grabbed his towel and the cooler. "Beats me, but we better get going. If Grandpa needs us, we can't help from here."

Claire tied on her sneakers and whistled for Reesha. "Come on, girl. Time to go."

When they reached the corrals ten minutes later, the five horses rescued that morning were grazing. The mare and colt were still missing and the pickup was gone. The kids ran into the kitchen, calling for their grandparents.

"Aunt Alice isn't here, either," said David. He tossed his pack on the table then turned on his two-way radio. "Hello, Grandpa? Come in please. It's David. Hello? Over."

A voice came from another room. The cousins looked at one another, puzzled. David clicked the dials, saying "over" each time then waited for a response. When they heard an echo down the hallway, they crept toward the noise.

"Not again," cried Claire. She tromped into Grandpa's study. There on the desk was his walkie-talkie. "The map's here too!"

"Rats!" said Jeff. "Grandpa must've brought these from the truck before heading out with Gram. He set this down and forgot."

"But if that was Riley calling, what was he doing here?" David wondered.

"My question exactly," said Jeff.

"Everything's neat and tidy," Claire said, "so it doesn't look like a thief busted in."

Suddenly they looked up. From the open window they heard the sound of hooves clopping along the dirt road. Claire stood on her tiptoes to see over the top of the café-curtain.

"Guys, you're not going to believe this."

11
A Real Cowboy

A man on a spotted horse rode into sight. He led a pinto mare by a rope tied to his saddle. A tiny colt, brown with patches of white like its mother, trotted alongside. Reesha darted out from the back porch to help. The little cow dog circled the newcomers, her head lower than her shoulders then she escorted them to the paddock.

The cousins watched from the window. The cowboy wore a checkered bandana around his nose and mouth to keep out the dust. They weren't able to see his face, but they recognized his hat: a white Stetson with braided leather around the crown.

"Riley! I thought he was never coming back," Claire cried.

"Me, too," said David. "I'll go talk to him."

"No, I'll go. I'm the oldest." Jeff headed for the door.

"I saw him first," said Claire, pulling Jeff's sleeve to keep him in the study. "I should be the one to question him. Grandpa thinks I'm a good detective, remember?"

Jeff peeled her fingers off his shirt. "He said that about all of us, and you're only nine."

"So?"

"*Sooo*, if Riley started the fire," said David, "he's definitely dangerous—"

"—and you're safer here," Jeff agreed.

Claire crossed her arms. "You guys aren't the boss of me."

While the threesome argued, the ranch hand jumped out of his saddle. He ushered the pintos and his appaloosa into the corral, and went in with them. He closed the gate. Then he led them to the water trough, which was an old bathtub next to a long-handled pump. Riley wandered among the herd, patting their flanks and stroking their cheeks. They nuzzled his palm for the carrot stubs he pulled from his pocket.

"If he's so dangerous, why do the horses like him?" Claire said. "Come on, boys, let's chat him up before he runs off again." She marched through the kitchen and out the back door with Reesha. The brothers hurried after her.

At the corral the cousins boosted themselves onto a rail, perching like three birds. They were happy to see that all six horses and the colt were safely home.

"Hello there, you kiddos." Riley lifted his hat in greeting and came over to them. His boots jingled from spurs around his heels. He spoke in a pleasant drawl. "I'm mighty glad to see y'all. Heard you were coming for a few weeks."

"We have questions," Claire began. But suddenly she felt shy facing their old friend. She guessed he'd been riding all day because the leather chaps over his jeans were dusty. He looked tired.

"Ask away. I'm listening," said Riley. He unstrapped his saddle and lifted it to hang over a fence. Two leather bags attached in front to the pommel, rattled with their contents.

"First," said Jeff, "are you all right? Were you hurt in the fire?"

"I'm fine, Jeff. Thank you for asking. But I'm deeply sorry the flames got out of control."

The cousins nudged one another.

"Why'd you do it?" asked David.

"The horses almost died!" Claire was near tears with this upsetting thought.

63

"I beg your pardon?" said Riley. "What are y'all talking about?"

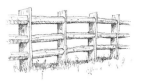

"Grandpa said you were mad at him," David answered.

"Then the next thing," said Jeff, "the barns were on fire and since you smoke cigarettes—"

Claire interrupted, "We're sorry, Riley, but it's too weird. You wanted a cellphone, and now it's missing."

"Only guilty people run away," said David.

"Is that so?" The cowboy regarded the cousins with sad eyes. Then he shook his head.

"We've known each other your whole lives. I was at your baptisms with your folks. I taught you how to ride and take care of the horses. Have I ever let you get hurt or scared?" Riley's voice rose with anger. "Have I?"

The children looked down at their feet. "No," they answered.

Riley opened the flaps of his saddlebags. His face twisted with a look of pain. He pulled out brushes and currycombs then handed them to the kids. "Make yourselves useful."

"Where'd you get these?" David asked.

Claire jumped in. "We mean, since the tack room and everything burned down."

64

Riley looked up at the sky. He took a deep breath. Then leaning toward them, he whispered, "I stole 'em."

The cousins' mouths popped open in disbelief.

He watched their shocked reactions then he raised an eyebrow. "Come on, you kiddos. My sister, Elaine, has a ranch up the road, remember? She loaned me some brushes so I can take care of the horses."

He began combing the pinto's tangled mane, but stopped. He looked at them again.

"*Seriously?* Y'all think I'm a thief? That I caused the fire? I love my job and would never do anything to hurt your family."

Jeff, David, and Claire fell silent. They brushed the ponies with long, thoughtful strokes, and kept glancing at the cowboy. They were ashamed for having assumed the worst of him.

Ten minutes passed.

Late afternoon sun slanted through the poplar trees that lined the road like sentries. Shade now touched the corral. Reesha scratched in the dirt for a cool spot and was resting, ears alert.

"I was upset by your grandfather's questions," Riley finally said. "Sometimes I need to be alone to sort things out. I came back to apologize for storming away, but saw flames along the row of stables."

He patted the mare and her colt. "Buddy and Reesha were nipping at these two, trying to get them out of their stall."

"Oh!" cried Claire.

"Well, finally it worked, but mom and baby panicked. They took off. I followed on my horse, chasing them into Bluebird Canyon." He paused.

"Poor little colt," Riley went on. "It was too exhausted to go another step. I found water then tied the mother to a tree. Slept under the stars. Took us all this morning to get to Elaine's place."

"Why didn't you call to let Grandpa know?"

"Claire, if I had a cellphone I most certainly would've done so. When I got to my sister's I used her phone, but there was no answer here. So while she fed the horses and they rested, I rode her bike over."

"So that explains why we didn't see your truck," said Jeff.

"Anyhow," Riley said, "no one was here. I found the walkie-talkie on your grandfather's desk, but reception was terrible, couldn't get through. I rode back to Elaine's."

"But yesterday when you were with Grandpa, why did you get so mad?" Jeff asked.

"Have y'all ever steamed up and worried about losing your temper? Didn't want to say something you'd regret later?"

Slowly the cousins nodded.

"Of course you have," said Riley. "We all have. And Claire, I've heard that redheads might stomp their foot a time or two. Am I right?"

She shook her head no. But the brothers answered for her. "*Oh, yeah.*"

The cowboy went to the trough and pumped fresh water. He filled his hat to take a drink then dumped it over his head to cool off. "It's been a long, hot day," he told them. "*Two* long days."

"I'm sorry I thought bad things about you, Riley," Claire said.

"Me, too," said David.

"We shouldn't have accused you. I'm really sorry." Jeff reached out to shake his hand.

But Riley turned away. He untied the wet bandana and stuffed it in his pocket. Without saying good-bye, he walked to his bunkhouse.

12
Another Development

Claire laid her cheek on the colt's withers. He was warm and smelled of hay and fresh air. She wrapped her arms around his neck. "I'm so happy the animals are all right," she told her cousins. "But I feel awful. About hurting Riley, I mean."

"Same here," said David. "We really blew it."

Jeff knocked the dust from his brush and returned it to the saddlebag. "I won't blame him if he never talks to us again."

"Oh, *yoo-hoo*, angels!" called Aunt Alice from the back porch. She waved to them, smiling, a frilly white apron around her waist. "Can you please give me a hand?"

Claire waved back. "Coming!" she cried. "Oh wow guys, I'm sooo glad we didn't accuse her."

"She would've been heartbroken," said David.

"It's probably the smartest thing we ever *didn't* do," said Jeff. He thought a moment. "But we've seen her take stuff, right? So she's still a suspect."

"Yeah," David said. "But if she's guilty, why is her own scarf missing?"

"Good question."

"Hmm," Claire answered. "Maybe Aunt Alice just *thinks* it's lost. You know how our parents always forget where they put the car keys? Then they find them in pockets or someplace like that?"

"Yeah, maybe that's it."

Jeff closed the flaps to the saddlebags then cinched them tight. Looking toward the ranch house he said, "Okay, let's be real careful with Aunt Alice. But I'm still weirded out with our biggest problem: Who started the fire and why?"

The kitchen had the good aroma of supper: grilled onions on the stove, and a cherry cobbler in the oven. The cousins set to work, glad to be distracted from their terrible mistake with Riley. Claire swept the floor. David tasted Aunt Alice's tomato vegetable soup that was cooking on the stove. Then he searched the cupboards for spices. Jeff crawled under the sink to mop the leaky faucet. He turned a valve and the dripping stopped.

Meanwhile their aunt filled two bowls with kibble, adding chopped apples and bananas. "I love to give the dogs their vitamins," she announced. She couldn't remember their names, so she called them by color. Setting the bowls on the floor she said, "Here you go, Little Red. And here's yours, Big Brown."

"Aunt Alice?" Claire said gently. "Have you found your scarf? We've kept an eye open, but haven't seen it."

"No, dear. It just vanished. And it was my favorite."

David concentrated on the chili. With a wild flurry he added dashes and spoonsful from the spice jars. "There, that should do it!"

"Aunt Alice," Jeff chimed in. "we'll keep looking, so don't worry."

She gave the cousins an adoring smile. "Such sweethearts you are. Dinner isn't for another hour. So while the soup simmers and the cobbler bakes—there's no sugar in it, by the way—could you please help with something else?"

"Of course," said Claire.

"In your grandpa's study, open the windows so it'll be cool this evening. He likes to read there late at night."

"On it!" David cried. He put the lid on the pot and turned the flame to low.

"Anything else we can do?" Jeff asked.

"Actually, yes. Something else has disappeared."

"What!" the brothers cried.

Claire stopped sweeping. She looked at her aunt. "Oh no! What is it?"

Aunt Alice put her hand in the pocket of her apron. A look of confusion crossed her face. "Uh, it's on the tip of my tongue. Hmm, I guess I'll tell you later, my angels."

"We'd really like to help you, Aunt Alice," said Jeff.

"I know you would, angel, so perhaps if—"

The cousins waited for her to finish her sentence."

The elderly woman smiled at them. "I'm sorry. Sometime I get lost in my head and can't find my way."

"It's alright, Aunt Alice," said Claire. "We're here for you."

"Thank you, dear. While you children are in the study, I'll think and think. It's something important, I remember that much. I need it every day, but it's gone."

13
The Crooked Floor

*T*he children opened windows in the study. They could hear Aunt Alice in the kitchen, setting plates and silverware on the table.

"What now?" Claire asked her cousins. "We were totally wrong about Riley and Aunt Alice."

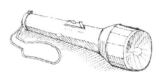

David opened his sketchbook. "You're not kidding," he said. "Time to cross them off our list of suspects."

"Okay, how about this, guys," said Jeff. "Things first went missing from Grandpa's office, so let's look around here. Maybe we'll find some clues."

The curtains fluttered from a breeze as they searched the book-filled room. When a sudden gust of wind rustled papers on the desk, the breeze also moved the cardboard tube. Ever so slowly, the map rolled to the edge then fell to the floor.

Claire bent to rescue it.

"Wait!" cried Jeff, grabbing her ponytail to stop her. "Ow!"

"I'm sorry Claire, but this gives me an idea. Check this out."

The cousins watched as the tube continued to roll. The floor sloped a bit because the ranch house was more than one hundred years old. Many of the floorboards had warped with age.

"Are you guys thinking what I'm thinking?" Jeff asked.

Claire put her hands on her hips and nodded. "Yep."

"Oh Buddy," Jeff called down the hallway to the kitchen. "Here boy."

And soon not one, but two dogs trotted into the study.

David held Reesha's collar so she would stay beside him.

"Okay, let's experiment," said Jeff. "Buddy, come!" He petted him then pointed to the map, which now had bumped into a chair. "Go get it, boy," he said.

Buddy looked at them with droopy eyes. He took his time considering the command then finally retrieved the tube. He dropped it on the oval rug where they stood.

"Hmm, weird," said Claire. "This morning only Reesha would fetch, but now he does, too. Wonder why."

David fiddled with the tag on the front of his shirt, thinking. "Something's different all right," he said.

Claire noticed the pen near some stationery. She rolled it on the floor to Buddy. His head whipped around as if he'd seen a mouse. He stopped it with his big paw then gently brought it to her in his mouth.

"Good boy." She hugged his thick neck. "Hey guys, maybe Buddy only picks up stuff with the scent of salami. When these things went missing at Christmas, I bet Grandpa had been snacking in here where it's warm."

David took out his pencil. On a new page of his sketchbook, he drew the Rottweiler with a map and pen. "Grandpa likes fresh air, even in winter, right?" he asked.

"Right," said Jeff.

"He leaves windows open and sometimes the kitchen door, right?" David continued.

"Right," answered Claire.

 "Soooo, when Grandpa left the room"—David now sketched a big smile on the dog—"he didn't know that wind would blow these things off his desk."

"Exactly!" Jeff laughed. His brown eyes were wide with excitement. "So Buddy swiped them and snuck out the back door to the bunkhouse."

"*Then*," said Claire, holding her idea finger in the air, "they rolled under my bunk where we found them yesterday. That floor is even more crooked than this one."

Jeff patted her on the shoulder. "We make a good team, cousin. That connects Buddy to the map and Dad's silver pen. He was the only dog here at Christmas."

"*And*," she went on, "if Buddy took the map, we don't need to worry about someone digging for treasure."

"Hey, you're right," David said. He flipped through his drawings. "Okay, so now we need to investigate the stolen iPhone."

Jeff said, "You know what, guys? I'm pretty sure Aunt Alice didn't take it. Remember how Grandpa said she has trouble working the TV remote? A cell phone is way more complicated."

"Good point," said David. "So let's go help her with dinner. Even if she has Alzheimer's maybe she'll remember what she forgot."

14
"Rotten Awful Miserable"

*W*hen the cousins returned to the kitchen, Aunt Alice was opening a window over the sink. A breeze began cooling the hot kitchen. "Well, look at that. Your grandparents just rode in from the trail."

"Yay!" Claire said. "I can't wait to tell them how the baby colt got home."

Jeff pointed to the corral. "I think they're about to find out," he said. David joined them at the window.

Gram and Grandpa draped their saddles and bridles over a rail. As they wiped down their tired horses, Riley strode out from his bunkhouse to greet them. After what appeared to be a pleasant conversation, he and Grandpa shook hands. Then Gram gave Riley a long hug. She gestured for him to come into the house, but he walked away.

*G*ram came into the house looking glum. "I can't believe Riley didn't want any dinner. He always joins us."

"Um, yeah," Claire said. Then she and the boys explained what happened and how they had accused Riley.

Grandpa listened to the children while washing his hands at the sink. Gram shook her head with disappointment. She said, "No wonder he doesn't want be here tonight."

"I don't blame him," said Jeff.

"We feel rotten awful miserable," Claire said, her voice shaky.

David wished he stood as tall as his brother, so he might feel braver. A moment passed. "We made a bad mistake," he finally admitted. "But, Grandpa, we've solved some of the mysteries here."

"Oh?"

"Yes, look." He went to a corner where he'd thrown his pack and returned with his sketchbook. He flipped through the pages. Then he drew a circle around Buddy and Reesha with a new label: POSSIBLE SUSPECTS.

Claire spoke up. "Grandpa, we figured out that every time you eat salami and crackers then touch something, Buddy and Reesha sneak in to lick off the flavor. Then, like with bones, they bury 'em. We just have to find where they've been digging."

"And since Riley smokes," Jeff said, "that's why we thought he could've started the fire. I mean by dropping a match."

Aunt Alice brought the pot of soup to the table. As she ladled it into large mugs, the kids continued with their theories.

Their grandparents listened. They waited for Alice to sit down then Grandpa bowed his head to say grace.

"Thank you, Lord, for our family and friends, and for this meal. Please help us always to be kind and to be generous with those in need. Amen."

"Amen," the others said.

Grandpa snapped his napkin into his lap then took a sip of soup. His eyes began to water. He coughed. "Couple of things you should know, children." He took a drink of iced tea then coughed again.

"Are you okay, Grandpa?" asked Claire.

He nodded. "First off," he said, taking another drink. "We've all been trying to get healthy around here. I plan to give up my pipe. And for your information Riley quit smoking months ago."

Claire's shoulders sagged. She gave a loud sigh. "Why didn't he tell us? I would've kept my mouth shut."

Gram raised her eyebrows. "Young lady, that's not a bad idea in any situation."

"*Second*," Grandpa went on, "I've cut salt out of my diet to help my blood pressure. I haven't eaten salami in ages. Gram here, wants me to be full of zip."

"But today out at the pond you told us it was your favorite," said Jeff.

"It is," Grandpa replied, "with a pile of salty crackers, my most favorite snack in the whole world. I just don't eat that stuff anymore, or sugar. It's funny how much better I feel."

David set down his pencil. "Well, there goes that theory."

Grandpa waved his hand to cool off his mouth. "Whew-ie," he said. "Hottest, pepper-iest, most interesting vegetable soup I ever did taste. Let me guess. You kids helped Aunt Alice?"

"Yep," said David. "There's a secret ingredient."

"I'll bet there is, Grandson." He finished his glass of tea then reached for Gram's. After a long swig Grandpa said, "I just can't put my finger on what it might be. Help me out, will you?"

80

David sat up straight. With a proud smile, he said, "Cinnamon red-hots!"

15
An Odd Phone Call

*A*fter supper, Gram carried the cobbler out to the front porch. She set the pan on a card table. The sun was just setting behind the mountains and the air was cooling off after the hot summer day. Crickets had begun their nightly serenade.

"Everyone, come," she called to the clatter of plates in the kitchen.

"It's too lovely an evening to be inside doing dishes. Jeff, grab a bunch of spoons, would you please? Thanks, dearie."

On the trellis overhead, roses were purple in the waning sunlight.

The kids, their grandparents, and Aunt Alice scooted up chairs. Without ceremony or napkins to catch the drippings, they dug in with their spoons. Quietly, Buddy and Reesha reported for duty, settling under the table. Soon the cobbler was finished and the dogs cleaned the floor.

Aunt Alice sighed with contentment. "I love how the crickets sound this time of year, don't you?"

"Totally," David agreed. "And they sure are loud tonight."

Jeff said, "Aunt Alice, you mentioned that something of yours disappeared?"

"Yes, angel. Now I remember. My big tube of lotion." She laughed good-naturedly and fingered the pearls around her neck. "The air is so dry, my hands get chapped. I need lots of moisturizer."

"My mom is the same way," Claire said. "We'll keep trying to find it for you."

"Oookay, I better get my pencil." David wiped his gooey hands on his shirt, which was still inside out. Then he went inside for his sketchbook.

Gram had carried the pan into the kitchen and was on the phone. She held her palm over the receiver and whispered, "I'll be out in a second."

On the porch by the glow of window light, David started drawing. Soon he had a sketch of Aunt Alice in flip-flops with a big smiley sun shining on her. He wrote STOLEN LOTION with a question mark. Just for fun, he added his grandfather in flowered bathing trunks.

Meanwhile, Gram brought out a tray of steaming mugs: herb tea for her sister and Grandpa, hot chocolate for the kids.

"Thanks, Gram!" they cried, immediately slurping the whipped cream.

83

After a moment Claire said, "That's weird."

"What's weird, honey?" said Grandpa.

"How crickets just stop sometimes. It's like they hear us talking and go quiet so they can eavesdrop."

"Ha!" David laughed. "They're spying. It's because they're genetically programmed—"

"You're just making that up," said Jeff.

"No, I'm not."

While the brothers debated insects, the night grew even cooler. Gram went inside for sweaters.

"There go the crickets again," Claire observed. "Watch, when Gram comes back, they'll be silent." She could see through the living room to the kitchen where her grandmother was on the phone.

When Gram came out with some blankets and sweaters, Grandpa said, "Del honey, who's that you keep calling?"

"Me," she answered.

"Huh?" they all said.

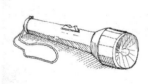

"I keep calling my cell, hoping to find it ringing nearby. It's only been lost a couple days so the battery should be good."

Claire jumped up from her chair. "Grandpa, remember you told us you were out here programming a new ring-tone—"

84

"—then you went in the house to help Aunt Alice with the TV," David said, finishing her sentence.

"But," Jeff continued, "when you came back, the phone was gone?"

"I do remember." Mr. Bridger took his unlit pipe from his pocket. He chewed on the stem, thinking.

"Grandfather," said Claire in a soft voice, "which ring-tone?"

"Well, I was trying to decide between a train whistle and a horn. Or something more peaceful."

"Something peaceful?" Jeff said. "Like crickets?"

Grandpa set his pipe on his knee. "Well, I'll be. Yes, boy, crickets."

"Grandmother," David yelled into the house. "Call your number again."

Gram went to the wall phone. Outside, the chorus of crickets returned.

The cousins listened, craning their necks to hear the location. Finally, they looked down. Jeff cried, "Right here, under the porch."

Claire ran inside to get their flashlights from their packs. Since she and David were the smallest, they crawled below the wooden slats of the porch. This time, the singing crickets grew louder. By the yellow beams of their lights, they found the cellphone buried in twigs.

Grandpa bent over the railing to se "My word. What's it doing there?"

"It had to have been Buddy," Claire said as she crawled out of the dirt. "He's always dusty after his nap."

"Well, I'll be."

"But Grandpa, why would he steal this?" Jeff asked. "You don't eat salty things anymore."

Mr. Bridger gazed out at the dark fields. A wall of speckled stars touched the horizon. "Hm," he said. "You detectives have a good point. There's a more serious question, however."

The cousins flipped through David's sketchbook.

Finally Claire raised her hand as if in school. "I know, I know! Aunt Alice's scarf. Buddy wouldn't steal that."

"Or her moisturizer," said Jeff.

David groaned with frustration. "Well, there goes another theory. Those are *her* things, not Grandpa's."

In the window light, Grandpa's face showed concern. "I'm most eager to solve how the fire started," he said. "If it happens again, we won't be able to call this Lucky Bridger Ranch."

16
Up in the Air

*I*n the bunkhouse the next morning, Claire's alarm clock clanged at 5:30. She dressed quickly inside her sleeping bag. In quiet grogginess, the boys found their shoes and sweatshirts.

It was still dark out. Reesha escorted the cousins to the ranch house where windows glowed with yellow light. A welcoming aroma of pancakes stirred their hunger.

"'Morning, dearies," Gram said when they came
into the kitchen. They went to the stove to hug her.
She looked spiffy in a chef's apron tied around her neck,
spatula in hand. "I'll join you in a minute. Pour
yourselves some fresh orange juice."

Grandpa was already at the table. He sprinkled
pepper onto his poached eggs then said, "What're you
kids up to? Any plans today?"

"We're still thinking about the fire," said Jeff, "and
we want to help you rebuild the stables."

"Sure you're up for it? Yesterday was pretty hectic
for you sleuths."

David held out his arm to flex his muscle. "We're
expert at hammering things."

"I'll bet you are," Grandpa said.

"And I'm good on the ladder," Claire offered.
"You saw how I climbed that tree."

"I certainly did, honey." He smiled at his
grandchildren then turned to the kitchen door. "Oh, hey
there Riley, come on in. Del's making your specialty."

"Just how you like it," Gram said. She scrambled
three eggs into a cast iron skillet. "And toast with
sliced tomatoes, coming up. Coffee's hot."

"Thank you, and good
morning to everyone." Riley
hung his Stetson on the hat rack
then pulled out a chair.

An awkward silence filled
the room.

The kids were embarrassed about how they had treated Riley. They glanced at one another across the table, worried that he would never forgive them. His spoon clinked against his mug as he stirred in milk. The marmalade that Grandpa scraped onto his toast made a skooshy sound. No one spoke. By the time Gram joined them with her pancake and bowl of yogurt, several moments had passed.

"About an hour ago," she said, breaking the quiet, "I went out to the corral. There was no moon, just starlight, but I could see that the horses were fine. Riley, thank you for putting a blanket on the colt last night."

"Yes, ma'am. Glad to do it."

Grandpa dipped his toast into the yolk of his eggs. Before taking a bite he said, "Riley, how about we build a row of lean-tos today? Already I have some volunteers."

"Mm," he replied between sips of coffee. "Might those volunteers be in this room?"

"They might be."

"Mm," Riley said again. He set his mug down. His face looked serious, but when he noticed the kids squirming with discomfort he softened. "I suppose y'all are ready to work hard today?"

"Are we ever!" Jeff burst out, relieved that their old friend was speaking to them.

"I'm in," said Claire.

"Me, too," said David.

"Good. That gives us time to rake up the ashes before the lumberyard opens."

*J*eff and David rode in the front seat of Riley's pickup. The big Rottweiler hung his head out the passenger window, his ears flying in the wind. Claire sat in the backseat with Reesha. She held an arm around her to keep her from sliding to the floor as Riley barreled down the bumpy dirt road. She liked looking out at the miles of fields and horse pastures.

Jeff pointed to a grove of aspen along the fence line. "Hey, there's a Mountain Bluebird. On that branch, see the bright blue?"

"That's because it's a boy," David declared. "The females are pale and kind of ugly."

"You're making that up," Claire said.

"Nope. I did a report in 3rd Grade. Also, it's the state bird for Idaho."

As the truck approached the tree, Claire leaned out her window for a good look. "Guess what guys, that's not a Mountain Bluebird."

"Then it's a blue jay," said David.

"Dude," said his older brother, "it's not even a bird. It's a pillow case or something that flew off a clothesline."

Claire interrupted. "Get your notebook, David."

"Okay, Miss Bossy, but why?"

"So you can X-out Aunt Alice's scarf. Riley, please stop the truck!"

"What!" the boys cried over the wind. The rattling truck was noisy as Riley pulled over.

"Be right back!" Claire jumped out and ran to the tree. She plucked the scarf from a low branch then returned to the back seat, yelling, "Score! I bet Aunt Alice dropped it and a breeze took it like a phantom. What d'you guys think?"

Jeff turned around to smile at his cousin. "I think you're pretty smart, Claire Posey, that's what I think."

"Me, too," said David, "even though you're just a kid."

"Thanks guys. Now we need to find Aunt Alice's lotion."

17

Busy, Busy

*T*wo hours later, Riley and the cousins were home from the lumberyard. Grandpa gave the kids thick work gloves like his so they wouldn't get splinters. They helped unload planks of wood that hung out the back of the pickup. Soon all were hammering nails, and the long sides of a lean-to took shape.

Claire appointed herself snack chairman and used the wheelbarrow to deliver refreshments. She rolled out a gallon jug of ice-cold water with cups, so no one would get too thirsty under the hot sun. She carted apples and granola bars, and also their backpacks. She liked the way the barrow pivoted on its front wheel. Hanging on to its handles, she could jog back and forth to the ranch house. It reminded her of pushing her doll carriage when she was little, but this was much more interesting.

Reesha watched the activities from under a shady tree But Buddy was busy. He dug and dug below the kitchen window, dirt flying behind his paws. One by one, he carried several items to the back porch.

First was a long-handled brush that Claire recognized as having come from the tack room before it burned down. He nudged it under a picnic table then returned to his digging spot. He brought a dishtowel then a potholder. Next came a red mitten covered in dirt.

When Claire saw him dig up what looked like a saltshaker, she worried the glass might cut him. "Here, boy, let me have that."

She whistled and held out her hand, but Buddy ignored her. He crept under the table, making a nest of his treasures. He wouldn't look at her. She went over to him and set a small yellow apple by his nose. His whiskers twitched. He sniffed. When he finally opened his mouth to taste the apple, out rolled a slobbery tube of lotion.

"Aha!" Claire cried. She wiped the goo on her jeans to read the label. "Hey guys, guess what I found! Tropic Mama Skin Cream. It's got banana, pineapple, and coconut scent."

She scooped Buddy's loot into the wheelbarrow then pushed it at a fast trot over to her grandfather. Reesha heard the excitement in Claire's voice and ran beside her, barking and barking.

Buddy trotted after them. His big head looked into the barrow as if to keep track of his things.

"Well, I'll be," Grandpa laughed. "This brush disappeared a month ago. And Alice has been knitting red mittens forever. I wonder where her others are hidden."

Jeff and David set their hammers in the dirt to give Claire high-fives. David said, "You should be an FBI agent."

"Thank you. Well anyway, I've been thinking," she said.

Again Grandpa laughed. "I'm sure you have been, honey."

"Okay," she started. "Aunt Alice puts bananas and apples in Buddy's dish, so we know he likes fruit. He must've smelled this lotion and that's why he took it."

Jeff rolled the tube in his hands. "Grandpa, do you ever use this in the winter?"

"Well yes Grandson, I do. My fingers get cracked from working out in the cold. Even with gloves on."

"You don't eat salami any more," David said, following his brother's thought, "but your hands smell like tropical fruit. Ha! Grandpa, you're the phantom of Hidden Horse Ranch!"

Claire bounced on her toes, thrilled by their discovery. "And Grandpa, you said Buddy likes to hang out at the stables?"

"Yes, honey."

"Last Christmas you were using your magnifying glass, right?" she asked.

"Yep. Was trying to read the guide to our DVD player. Blasted tiny print."

"So Grandpa," said Jeff, "when you weren't looking Buddy licked the handle. He liked the taste of Tropic Mama so he snuck it out to the barn——"

"——he just wanted to have a good chew while visiting the horses," said David. "He probably left it in the hay and went on to another project."

"Like stealing this brush," Claire said.

Jeff looked up at the bright blue sky, shading his eyes with both his hands. He thought a moment then said, "So a few days ago the hot sun shined into the stable, onto the lens, magnifying the heat——"

"——and sparked the hay!" David was practically shouting. "Like we did by accident, on Lost Island."

"Grandfather," said Claire, rushing into his arms. "Buddy didn't mean to start the fire. Please don't punish him."

He hugged her. "I won't honey. He's just a busy, busy dog."

Riley rolled up his measuring tape and walked over to them.

"Mr. Bridger, you know I keep the stalls clean. Sometimes I find a bone or old shoe buried in the straw where Buddy likes to take naps."

"You didn't notice the magnifying glass?" David asked.

"Nope. It's big enough that my rake surely would've found it. I'm very careful."

"Of course you are, Riley. You always have been," said Grandpa.

The cousins were quiet. Finally Jeff said, "Then Buddy must've have dug it up from another hiding place. He brought it to the horses a few days ago."

"—*after* you cleaned the barn, Riley," said Claire. "That's why you didn't see it. It wasn't there."

Grandpa clamped the man's shoulder. "I'm grateful for all you do around here, Riley. Especially finding Alice's horse and the little one."

"Aunt Alice has a horse?" David cried.

Claire looked at David and he looked at his brother. They remembered something else they wanted to ask.

18
The Wild Ones

A sycamore tree shaded the work area. As the cousins stood with their grandfather among the pieces of sawed lumber, Jeff braved the question. "Grandpa, does Aunt Alice have Alzheimer's?"

"We saw her take tuna and hide it in her purse," David blurted. He rushed to the wheelbarrow for his sketchbook. "Grandpa, there're still a couple things we want to cross off our list."

Mr. Bridger sat on a bench in the shade. It had been carved from a log and curved like a couch. "Let's rest a bit, kids, and have a cold drink. I think you're old enough now to know about Aunt Alice."

"Know what, Grandfather?" Claire asked. She poured him a cup of water then one for herself and the boys.

He pointed to the porch where it wrapped around to the front of the ranch house. The trellis of roses provided shade for the white wicker chairs where Gram and Alice were sitting.

Gram was reading, her feet propped on a stool. Her red cowboy boots matched the yarn of Aunt Alice's knitting. They seemed perfectly peaceful.

"I've know those two gals most of my life," Grandpa began. "They were beauties, yessir. Still are, in my opinion. To see them now, you'd never guess their nickname as kids."

"What was it?" the three said at once.

"The Wild Twins of Green Meadows," Grandpa answered. "Adele and Alice. They rode their horses up and down these canyons. They did barrel racing in rodeos. In high school, they were suspended for galloping across the football field. During a game. And it wasn't even half-time."

"Our grandmother was wild?" Jeff asked.

Grandpa chuckled. "Grandson, even old folks were young once."

"It's hard to believe they were trouble-makers," said David.

"Oh my, yes. But what a sight on horseback. Fringed buckskin jackets, red boots, and their golden hair flying from under their Stetsons. Whew-ie!"

98

"They were blond?" Claire asked.

"Like sunshine," he answered. He smiled with the memory, ruffling David's hair. "And like our boy here."

Claire squinted at the porch. She tried to picture the elderly ladies as teenagers. Though now dressed as opposites—one church fancy with short hair, the other rugged with a long braid—their faces were identical. And still pretty. Their wrinkles gave them an aged beauty. She turned back to her grandfather.

"Something happened, didn't it Grandpa?"

"I'm afraid so, honey."

He took a deep breath.

"It was a blistering hot day in June, like today. Alice and Adele ditched school. They were sixteen and wanted to show off for some boys—I was one of them—so on horseback they began jumping fences."

"Like the fences around this ranch?" said David.

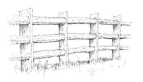 "Exactly. So Del made the first few jumps in beautiful form. But when Alice followed, a rattlesnake hissed from the trail.

"Those things are everywhere in heat like this. Anyhow, her horse spooked and threw her. Alice fell hard, hit her head."

The cousins listened, quiet, as if holding their breaths.

Reesha and Buddy moved from their spot in the shade to sit closer to the kids. Heads on their paws, they appeared to be listening, too.

"Then what?" Claire said.

"Well, terrible injuries. We weren't sure she'd pull through, but she did. Alice is tough."

"Is that why she can't remember our names?" Jeff asked.

"That's right. There're many things she does well, though, such as cook and knit."

"Does she ride that little pinto, too?" asked David.

Grandpa shook his head. His face looked sad. "Since the accident—it's been years and years now— she won't go near the corral. Won't wear jeans or boots. But your grandmother insists we keep a gentle mare in case Alice changes her mind."

Claire beamed. "Some day she might!"

"Yes, honey, that's our hope. At least so she can remember how happy it made her to pet and brush her own horse."

"But why does she raid your cupboards?" Jeff asked.

David blurted, "Yeah, she's like a pirate!"

Now Grandpa laughed. "It's odd, I know, but for years we've shopped for Aunt Alice. We tell her to help herself and she always puts everything back."

"So she can feel independent?" said Jeff.

"You kids are smart. Yep, that about sums it up. She's getting a bit more foggy so that's why we feel better about her living with us now."

David propped his sketchbook in the crook of his arm. He drew a big heart over Aunt Alice then closed the pages. "So the strange man who answered her phone call, she probably just misdialed, right?"

"Yes, Grandson. Happens a lot."

19
Deputies

*M*oments later, a red truck turned from the road to the ranch house. It drove up the long driveway, its tires crunching over the gravel. Green Meadows Fire Department was painted on its door.

"'Afternoon, inspector," said Grandpa when Mr. Luna stepped out with his clipboard. A canvas bag hung from his shoulder. They shook hands.

"Good to see you, Mr. Bridger. Just wanted to give you our final report."

"Thank you," said Grandpa. "We were wrapping things up here ourselves. I'm sure the fire was an accident."

"The chief and I agree," said the inspector. "Spontaneous combustion."

Grandpa said, "Kids, tell Mr. Luna your reasoning."

One by one, Jeff, David and Claire explained their theory. When they described the journey of the magnifying glass, they looked over at Buddy. The Rottweiler lay in the shade of the wheelbarrow. He appeared to be guarding it.

"Makes sense to me," said Mr. Luna. "Last August, an old trapper's cabin burned down. Squirrels had built nests in the loft, full of dried leaves and twigs."

"Was it a hot day with no clouds in the sky?" asked Jeff.

"Indeed it was. And there was no shade because loggers had recently cut a clearing."

"So the sun was stronger?" David said.

"Correct. Rays shining through the glass of a broken window sparked one of the nests and *pfft*. Flames spread as if lit by a match."

Mr. Luna opened his canvas bag. "But I'm also here for another reason. I heard about the skeleton found on Lost Island earlier this summer. The Cabin Creek paper said three children solved the mystery."

Claire raised her hand, but quickly put it in her pocket. She didn't want to boast. While Jeff opened his mouth to do exactly that, David yelled, "That was us!"

Mr. Luna smiled. "I thought so. Well," he said, pulling three ball caps and three T-shirts from his bag, "the guys and I want to say thank you for being good citizens. Try these on."

The caps and shirts were navy blue with the fire department logo. Embroidered above a miniature fire truck were the words, *Junior Deputies*."

"Wow, thanks!" they said.

The inspector shook hands with each of them. "Keep up the good work. Maybe some day one of you will have my job."

"On that note," said Grandpa, "what say we all go in and make lunch? Mr. Luna, we'd love for you to join us."

"Yeah!" the cousins cried.

"Don't mind if I do. Very kind of you."

Just then Aunt Alice stepped from the front porch carrying her basket of red yarn. She held up a newly knit mitten and waved it at Claire. "Yoo-hoo angel, this is for you."

Claire ran to her with an enthusiastic hug. "It's perfect. I love it, Aunt Alice. Thank you."

Grandpa turned to Riley and said, "Want to stir up your famous tuna salad? As you know, it's Alice's favorite. You'll make her day."

"You've got it, Mr. Bridger." The cowboy whistled for the dogs.

Reesha fell in step with the group, but not Buddy.

The big brown dog got up from the shade to look in the wheelbarrow. As if giving the matter serious thought, he grabbed the dishtowel. Then ignoring Riley's whistle he trotted away with it, on to a new project.

THE END

If you liked this *Cabin Creek Mystery*, turn the page for a sneak peek of others!

Cabin Creek #8:

The Case of the Spying Drone

1
An Early Start

*T*he Western Cafe opened before dawn. Ten-year-old Claire Posey helped her parents post the breakfast menu while looking out at the lake. It was beautiful this early, the water glowing pink from the sunrise.

"Mom, Dad, here they come!" she said, excitement in her voice. She could see her cousins on the sidewalk with their backpacks and sleeping bags. Jeff Bridger, thirteen, and David Bridger, eleven, carried a duffel between them with their tent and fishing gear.

When they entered the cafe a tiny bell jingled over the door. "Hi Aunt Lilly. Hi Uncle Wyatt," the brothers called.

"'Morning, boys. Your favorite is almost ready." Uncle Wyatt stood behind the grill making French toast. He wore his usual cowboy hat and chef's apron.

Aunt Lilly came from the kitchen. She was plump and pretty. She had the same green eyes and red hair as her daughter's, but her hair was short and curled at her cheeks.

She swept her nephews into a hug. "I see you're ready for your big adventure. I'll bring you some orange juice."

Lilly and Wyatt Posey owned this popular cafe in the mountain town of Cabin Creek. A neon sign blinked WELCOME FRIENDS, FREE WI-FI.

The brothers set their bags by the fireplace and warmed their hands. It was cold for spring. Their mother had dropped them off on her way to work at the Veterinary Hospital.

"Good girl, Yum-Yum," they said to Claire's little white poodle who occupied one of the cozy chairs. She had yellow bows on her ears and wore a purple sweater that matched Claire's. Her dainty paws had blue nail polish, also matching Claire's.

The three cousins went to the window where they could watch the quiet street.

Jeff said, "Any minute now."

"They're never late," said David.

Just then, a pickup truck pulled up front and parked in the space marked, *Reserved for Family*. Out stepped an elderly man in a baseball cap. His white beard framed his face.

When he entered the cafe Yum-Yum jumped down from her chair to greet him with a wagging tail. "Here you go Miss Fancy Pants," he said, slipping her a treat from his pocket.

"Mr. Wellback!" the kids cried. His real name was Gus Penny, but they called him Mr. Wellback because of how he began his stories.

"What're you whippersnappers doing up so early? I was hoping to have a cup of coffee in peace." He broke into a grin and shook hands with the brothers.

Claire leaned into his arm for a hug. He was like a grandpa to the children.

"Hello there, pumpkin," he said. "'Morning, Lilly. 'Morning, Wyatt. Those cinnamon rolls sure smell good. Ah, look who's here." He pointed outside.

A little red hybrid zipped into the spot by his pickup. The roof rack held an ice chest and a duffel bag. Their friend, Ariel, strode into the cafe.

112

"Hey everyone!" Her curly brown hair hung through the back of her cap in a loose ponytail. The sleeve of her sweatshirt had a logo from her university: College of Veterinary Science.

Ariel had invited Jeff, David, Claire, and Mr. Wellback to help research wildlife in the area. The five often went camping together. Now it was spring break, most of the snow had melted and Ariel had promised a surprise.

She drew in a deep breath. "That coffee smells good. Oh thank you, Mrs. Posey."

Aunt Lilly handed her a steaming mug then gestured to a booth with a view of the lake. "Your favorite table, everyone," she said. "Be right back."

As the five scooted into the booth David asked, with eagerness, "Did you bring it?"

"Sure did, buddy."

"When can we see it?"

Ariel smiled then took an appreciate sip of her coffee. She answered, "Soon as we get to the campground. I can't wait to show you."

#1 THE SECRET OF ROBBER'S CAVE

Lost Island was off limits--until now. Jeff and David are going to the desert island to search for clues. And hidden treasure! Town legend tells of a robber and a secret cave, but the brothers have to piece the truth together. With the help of their cousin, Claire, they'll get to the bottom of the mystery, no matter what they have to dig up.

#2 CLUE AT THE BOTTOM OF THE LAKE

It's the middle of the night when Jeff spots someone dumping a large bundle into the lake. It's too dark to identify anyone--or anything. But the cousins immediately suspect foul play, and plunge right into the mystery. Before they know it, the kids of Cabin Creek are in too deep. Everyone is a suspect--and the cousins are all in danger.

#3 THE LEGEND OF SKULL CLIFF

When a camper disappears from the dangerous lookout at Skull Cliff, the cousins wonder if it is the old town curse at work. Then the police discover a ransom note, and everyone is in search of a kidnaper. But Jeff, David, and Claire can't make the clues fit. Was the bossy boy from the city kidnapped, or did something even spookier take place on Skull Cliff.

#4 THE HAUNTING OF HILLSIDE SCHOOL

When a girl's face appears, then disappears, outside a window of their spooky old schoolhouse, the cousins think they've seen a ghost. More strange clues--piano music lilting through empty halls, a secret passageway, and an old portrait that looks like the girl from the window--make Jeff, David, and Claire begin to wonder: Is their school just spooky, or could it be ... haunted?

#5 THE BLIZZARD ON BLUE MOUNTAIN

Jeff, David, and Claire love their winter break jobs at the ski chalet on Blue Mountain, where they get to snowboard and go sledding between shifts of cleaning and tending to the grounds. But when things start going missing from the chalet, the cousins find themselves prime suspects. Can they solve the mystery before they get ski-lifted out of their winter wonderland? Or will trying to solve the case make them the frosty culprit's next target?

#6 THE SECRET OF THE JUNKYARD SHADOW

The cousins discover a mysterious stranger sneaking into the local dump. When bikes, toasters, and other items disappear all over town, they begin to suspect he might be up to no good. But when these items show up again, fixed and freshly painted, Jeff, David, and Claire are confused. What kind of thief repairs and returns his stolen goods?

#7 THE PHANTOM OF HIDDEN HORSE RANCH

During summer vacation the cousins are excited to visit their grandparents on Hidden Horse Ranch. They get to sleep in a bunkhouse, swim in a pond with a rope swing, and ride horses any time they want. But they arrive to find that a mysterious fire has destroyed the stables, and the herd has escaped into the nearby canyons. Also troubling, valuable objects have been disappearing from the ranch house. As Jeff, David, and Claire follow clues and suspects, they keep running into dead-ends and wonder if the ranch has a phantom.

#8 THE CASE OF THE SPYING DRONE

During spring break, college student Ariel (from #3, *The Legend of Skull Cliff*), takes the cousins and family friend, Mr. Wellback, camping as her assistants: She has grant money to study wildlife with a drone. But when someone breaks into their tents and steals Claire's diary and David's sketchbook, the cousins feel they're being watched. And when a different drone hovers while they're fishing, the kids set out to investigate who is spying on them, and why?

About the Author

*K*ristiana Gregory's popular *Cabin Creek Mysteries* are from stories she told her sons where they were little and needed a bribe to go to bed. All she needed to say was, "Do you guys want to hear a Jeff and David story?" and *boom*, they were there. She is working on her next mystery, which continues the cousins' adventures in the rugged American West.

Kristiana grew up in Manhattan Beach, California, two blocks from the ocean and has always loved to make up stories. Her first rejection letter at age eleven was for a poem she wrote in class when she was supposed to be doing a math assignment. She's had a myriad of odd jobs: telephone operator, lifeguard, camp counselor, reporter, book reviewer & columnist for the Los Angeles Times, and finally author.

Jenny of the Tetons (Harcourt) won the Golden Kite Award in 1989 and was the first of two-dozen historical novels for middle-grade readers.

Bronte's Book Club is set in a town by the sea and is inspired by her own childhood and the girls' book club she led for several years.

Nugget: The Wildest, Most Heartbreakin'est Mining Camp in the West takes place in an Idaho mining camp of 1866, based on the song, "My Darling Clementine." It was chosen as the Idaho book for the 2010 National Book Festival, sponsored by the Library of Congress: honorary Chairs were President Barack Obama and First Lady Michelle Obama. Kristiana's most recent title in Scholastic's Dear America series is *Cannons At Dawn*, a sequel to the best-selling *The Winter of Red Snow*, which was made into a movie for the HBO Family Channel.

Her memoir, *Longhand: One Writer's Journey,* reveals behind-the-scenes of children's publishing, and the origin of ideas.

120

Kristiana and her husband live in Idaho with their golden retriever, Poppy. Their two adult sons visit often. In her spare time she loves to swim, hike, read, do yoga, look at clouds, and hang out with friends.

For a complete list of Kristiana's books please visit her website: kristianagregory.com

Acknowledgments

I'm very grateful to my husband, Kip, and our sons Gregory and Cody Rutty, for encouraging me to take risks and for patiently reading every single manuscript multiple times, and offering eagle-eye criticism.

Thanks especially to Cody for his cover photo and design, and interior artwork.
The Phantom of Hidden Horse Ranch is dedicated to these guys!

I'm also grateful to the Shari's gang, for our coffee shop discussions and their critiques as *Hidden Horse* grew from an idea into a finished manuscript. Lots of pie and herb tea! Thank you Leslie Gorin, Elisabeth Sharp McKetta, and Sarah Tregay for your honesty and friendship.